Alan Blackwood

SNAP SHOTS

Limited Special Edition. No. 19 of 25 paperbacks

AUSTIN MACAULEY PUBLISHERS™

LONDON • CAMBRIDGE • NEW YORK • SHARJAH

Alan Blackwood was in the book publishing business for most of his working life. He is also the author of many books and features on music, including a biography of the famous conductor Sir Thomas Beecham. More recently he has turned to fiction, with a novel, *Writer's Cramp* and *Pot Shots*, a collection of short stories. *Snap Shots* is his second essay in this medium.

Alan Blackwood

SNAP SHOTS

AUSTIN MACAULEY PUBLISHERS™

LONDON • CAMBRIDGE • NEW YORK • SHARJAH

ISBN 9781528920346 (Paperback)
ISBN 9781528968560 (ePub e-book)

www.austinmacauley.com

First Published (2019)
Austin Macauley Publishers Ltd
25 Canada Square
Canary Wharf
London
E14 5LQ

CONTENTS

TWO'S COMPANY

'MAY I?' She sat down across the table with a silken kiss of her legs and raised her glass. 'Cheers!'

The ship began to roll with the open sea. 'I love going places, don't you?'

'Not at night,' I said. Water and darkness. Like crossing the river Lethe.

The mascara, the false eyelashes, gave her the wide-eyed gaze of a doll. 'Are you a writer, or something?'

'Sort of.'

'It must be wonderful to write.' She watched the lights of the ferry going the other way. 'Ships that pass in the night,' she added dreamily.

A distant beam of light swung in a lazy arc. The French coast. 'Hasn't the time gone quickly!?' She smiled over my shoulder. 'Alright, darling?' Bill had to take his seasick pill and lie down.

On the car deck the names Bill and Sandra were stuck over the top of their windscreen. Then we were off in a blue haze of exhaust.

Ships that pass in the night.

CAT FLAP

LIKE waiting for a pot to boil, the phone will never ring as long as you wait. The front door answerphone buzzed instead.

A woman asked if she could leave a notice with us about a missing cat. She waited downstairs, wrapped up against the wind under a sky as hard and grey as pumice. Lost, said her sad notice, above a colour photograph of a furry little face, startled perhaps by the flash of the camera. Her name was Biscuit.

'Poor little Biscuit,' I said. But the woman had already gone, too cold to hang about.

A change in the weather brought clouds and rain, or tears to trickle down all those other pictures of the same furry little face, stuck on fences and around lampposts.

'Any luck?' On the way to the shops I'm sure it was the same woman, looking a lot better in plastic mac and wellies. 'Biscuit,' I reminded her. She frowned and hurried on.

Too wet to hang about.

SEA FEVER

O N Ocean Beach, fugitive rainbows danced about the tumbling surf, legions of tiny birds ran comically up and down the gleaming wet apron of the sea with each wave, and something on the sand had attracted a small crowd.

The downward slit of the mouth, the tail fin shaped like a cutlass, they'd found a young shark stranded on the beach which they were daring to touch and prod.

'Amazing creatures,' I said, 'no real bone just muscle to give them more strength, skin not scales for extra speed through the water, and fins that could turn them on a dime.'

So saying I boldly picked up the shark in both hands, strode into the waves, never mind my trousers, and cast him back into the sea. My good turn for the day, for as long as it lasted. Returning on my walk he was washed up again, too weak or too sick to swim against the tide.

Voracious predator he'd never grow up to be. Amen.

STILL LIFE

'I dreamt of those sparrows,' Carol said, the flush of last night's wine still on her. She'd had a tough time of late and this was her first holiday in years.

They'd be the ones flitting about the nave at Vezelay. We didn't expect to find birds in a church in our squeaky clean age, but what could be more natural, the commonplace and the numinous, made one. Like the pilgrims who gathered there a thousand years ago, a scruffy noisy crowd one moment, awestruck, the next. By the bells and by the image of the Risen Christ at the entrance to that wonderful nave.

'We've lost our sense of wonder,' I said, just as the line of grey-blue hills parted to reveal our first vineyard, the young shoots of vines calling down the sun.

Carol sat up. We turned a corner and sprawled across the road was the mangled body of a fox or hare. 'Oh God!' She buried her face in her hands.

Sometimes you just can't win.

CHILLED OUT

WITH a gust of steam and Brussels sprouts, Adam burst out of the kitchen and out of the house, slamming the front door behind him.

Christmas made no difference. Roberta and Adam, mother and son, didn't get on, and that was that. I gave it another couple of minutes, drained my sherry glass, wished Roberta a happy one, and departed with a little less fuss.

The deepening murk of afternoon threw into relief other brightly lit rooms and scenes of seasonal fun and games. And one that was more like a tableau. A large dining table was abandoned to the detritus of a festive meal, spent crackers, paper streamers, orange peel, nut shells, and old Granddad, fallen forward in his chair with his paper hat still on, fast asleep face down in his plum pudding and custard.

Someone else, hands thrust deep into his trouser pockets for warmth, had just joined me.

I turned to Adam. 'Says it all, really.'

PUNCH DRUNK

RITA sat Mr Punch in a chair, red pugnacious face and hump at one end, spindly legs at the other, and not much in between till someone shoved a hand up his backside.

Sam's, that is. With his pitch in Covent Garden he'd been a big help with the book I was writing about Punch and Judy, letting me in on the secret of his swazzle, the item he stuck in his mouth to get the funny voice ('That's the way to do it!'). A shame he had to leave town in such a rush, asking me to let Rita have his puppets.

She next picked up the Hangman holding his little wooden gibbet, and with a practised twist and a tug, pulled off his head. Stuffed into the neck was a wad of banknotes. She raised her glass. 'Here's to old Sam!'

'Sam,' I echoed, spilling gin on the sofa.

At her front door she tucked a banknote inside my shirt. 'For services rendered,' she whispered, daylight exposing the grey roots of her hair.

KILLING TIME

WHOEVER said it was better to travel hopefully than to arrive, was bang on. After six hours on the road, across blistering desert and down eight-lane highways, we pulled up by a grubby fringe of sand and a trash can.

First things first. Emily rushed off to find a loo while I cooled my feet in the sea and let nature take its course that way.

An aircraft caught the declining sun as it climbed over the ocean, turned and headed back towards the land. Others had done the same, but there was something about that one.

Emily thought so too. 'I *knew* we should have checked straight in.' She stepped back as the next little wave licked a few more inches up the sand. '"Time to kill," you said. Well, I reckon we've got about twenty-four hours of it now.'

Lights began to twinkle up the hill towards Sunset Boulevard. 'Are you going to stay out there all night?'

Just now, we had all this time to kill.

SOLO TURN

SEPTEMBER in the Rain sounded so much better on the Bechstein grand that stood in a corner of the hospital reception area. They let me have a go on it whenever I showed up.

'You play beautifully.' I turned around and nearly fell off the piano stool. It was the miserable old girl who'd shouted me down in Sainsbury's. I wonder what she was in for. A new face perhaps. At any rate, with those pebble glasses and that myopia I don't suppose she recognised me. 'Are you a concert pianist?' she asked.

'Not quite,' I smiled modestly, 'but I might have a go at the opening Prelude in C major from Bach's Forty-Eight, with its gentle progression of arpeggios or broken chords.'

I'd never played it better. The usual hospital commotion, the rattle of trolleys, PA announcements, the noise of the coffee dispenser, faded right away.

'Thank you,' she said softly at the end of it and tried a smile of her own.

HIGH NOON

THE large bell resting in the basement of the old Courthouse commemorated the time when there was a bell foundry down there. A small hammer on a chain invited you to strike it. 'Don't,' Judy said. 'Someone might hear you.'

Upstairs was the rest of the story. There, under glass, was Wyatt Earp's very own six-shooter, a faded sepia photograph of dentist, gambler and gunfighter Doc Holliday, pictured with his girlfriend Big Nose Kate, and a contemporary newspaper account of the Gunfight at the OK Corral, apparently all done and dusted in under thirty seconds. 'Come on,' Judy said.

Upstairs again was the old courtroom itself, preserved just as it must have been in those riotous days and how you saw it in some of those Western movies, while down below in the sun-baked courtyard was the four-poster gallows. They didn't hang about back then.

'Let's go,' Judy said, not in the mood for jokes.

PAPER TIGER

TIPPOO'S Tiger, a prize exhibit in the Victoria and Albert museum, had inspired Richard to write his book.

This mechanical wonder, that growled as it dug its claws into a red-coated soldier, had once belonged to the Sultan Tippoo of Mysore, who was killed fighting the army of the British East India Company. I'd watched Richard go bald and myopic as he wrestled with his account of the gallant Sultan's life and times, filling every inch of space in his tiny flat with books and photocopies, maps and pictures, piles of correspondence and stacks of typescript.

That still left, up on his wall, the old poster for a production of *King Lear*, with his name proudly included in the cast. Someone else in that cast list was now a star of stage and screen. It hadn't happened for him.

Richard reached for my bottle on the floor, where the lino curled up at the edges. 'I mean,' he said, 'what have I got to lose?'

Not his hair, I guess.

MONKEY NUTS

THE wind, the towering granite cliffs, the sea. It might almost be Cornwall or Brittany, with the mortally wounded Tristan waiting among those ruins for a sign of Isolde's ship.

Hang on. Not at eight degrees south of the equator, and Australia somewhere over those shark-ridden waters. We'd come to see the ruined temple with the sacred monkeys, and already feeding them was the woman from the bus who kept tossing back her hair to sneak another glance at the mystery man behind his silver-tinted glasses. Swedish perhaps with such soft pale hair.

I took off the glasses to treat her to a smile. A simian hand snatched them from my grasp. A sacred sphincter disappeared behind a heap of rocks.

'Talk about cheeky monkey!' she bawled, and everyone else from the bus turned around. I hid behind another pair of dark glasses, and one of the plastic eyepieces fell straight out.

'Be seein' yer, Lord Nelson!'

FAG END

CYRIL was like a headhunter's trophy; the grey shrunken face with the rictus of a grin and a few tufts of hair.

That's what forty fags a day for forty years had done for him. They'd also kippered and cured him against all infection. He was as indestructible as a flea and as difficult to brush off.

'Hi there!' I tucked myself in next to Anthea over by the door. 'Good party!' Her face was no oil painting but the rest of her I fancied something rotten.

Toying with his next cigarette, Cyril bobbed up between us. Christ, was there no escape. And where had Anthea gone?

Outside in the bleak courtyard I could at least breathe again and at the corner of the road jumped thankfully aboard a bus.

Cyril hopped on behind me. He flashed his freedom pass, sat down by my side and fiddled with his hearing aid. 'How far are you going?' he asked.

All the way with Anthea, given half a bleedin' chance.

SOUTHERN BELLE

THE Mardi Gras was over. A few shrivelled balloons still lolled from balconies, and in Jackson Square a solitary black man blew a few tuneless notes on a saxophone, a chilly requiem for the soul of jazz.

It was warmer on the bus. 'It's hot in here!' The driver glanced nervously at the old girl on the back seats as we pulled out of the station. Nutty but harmless, her crackling voice soon became a counterpoint to the whack of vulcanised rubber on road.

Biloxi, Pascagoula, Montgomery, Alabama, for coffee and donuts at some ungodly hour of the night, then on towards an unforgiving dawn. In so far as any of us slept, I don't think she did.

'Where are we now?' The Lincoln Memorial, after thirty-one hours.

At the depot she squatted by the empty baggage hold, snowflakes melting in her iron-grey hair. 'Where's my valise?'

Try A Streetcar Named Desire.

BLUE EYES

WITH his lovely thick coat of grey hair Mr Smoky rolled over when he saw me, a sure sign of trust.

Not like Blue Eyes, diving for cover beneath the nearest parked car or disappearing back into the garden of that empty house round the corner.

Jungle was more like it, where Blue Eyes, like one of the artist Henri Rousseau's fabulous tigers, might suddenly stare out at you with eyes that were almost the biggest things about her.

So where was she when they started clearing the place? Why, sitting by the front door preening herself in the sun and waiting for someone to return.

It's flowers again in the garden and curtains in the windows. But that's not Blue Eyes dozing in the same sunny spot. A bit like her, but much too well groomed.

Still, she was happy for a week or two. Which is as good as it gets for most of us.

CURTAIN CALL

ANOTHER first night, and Tony as Canon Chasuble elbowed his way back to the bar with a painful dig in the ribs for Peter, who made an exquisite Algernon. Jeremy, the director, and Peter's good friend, gripped his glass. He played rugby too.

Julia fiddled with Lady Bracknell's wig and pressed my hand. 'See you round the car park in ten minutes.'

So why, I wondered, all the bitchiness behind the smiling curtain calls? And was it worse among amateurs who felt they'd missed their true vocation?

Coming up the path to the car park, someone still in dog collar and gaiters tripped and fell in a puddle. Someone else giggled. Jeremy emerged from the shadows.

Julie tugged at her safety belt. 'Let's go.' We drove into a cosy world of large detached houses, gentrified pubs, and a church that flew the flag of St. George.

St. George for England! St. Pancras for Scotland! A good old chestnut for Tony in the Tudor Players' Christmas pantomime.

If he still had his teeth.

VIA CRUCIS

THE cypresses in the cemetery, grown old and ample on the compost of death, swayed and groaned before the mistral, the fierce, bone-dry wind that sometimes blew in those parts.

Never mind, it was the chapel we'd come to see. As a man of the cloth I thought David might be interested, and Jessica, of course.

The heavy oak door slammed shut behind us, and the sudden silence was awesome. A faint bluish light from one small east window fell like a tear upon the flagstones and a few benches were drawn up before the bare white altar. We breathed in the smell of cold stone. Jessica said, 'This place gives me the creeps.'

So what about the large iron crucifix hanging from my wall that I'd rescued from the cemetery dump. It must have belonged to some lost soul. 'David,' Jessica said, 'it's time we made a move.'

From their car window she shouted, 'We'll pray for you,' as the mistral carried them off in a cloud of dust.

EYE WITNESS

E DWARD'S dark glasses, romantic and mysterious, were aimed at the Polish waitress.

She was his type, he said, as we sat down to our working lunch and turned to *The Great Composers,* his latest mail order project. 'There'll be more work than you can shake a fist at!' Edward (don't ever call him Ted) spoke fast but softly with the hint of a transatlantic accent that could be very persuasive. 'Tchaikovsky was queer, wasn't he?'

'Yes,' I replied, 'and his marriage was a disaster.' The dark glasses gave nothing away, but Edward had been through more marriages than I could shake a fist at. 'It was always some little thing,' he confessed.

The Polish waitress handed us the wine list with a cool indifference. Edward lowered the dark glasses just enough to scan her and it, with one eye only. The other was black and blue and shut tight.

One of those little things, I supposed, as we settled for the Nuits Saint Georges.

NIGHT WATCH

WHEN I climbed the stairs, heaps of dead wasps lay like the fallen in battle on the bedroom floor. Others wandered up and down the windows, to fall in their turn.

In the stifling silence of the house, there came a soft but ceaseless rustling and nibbling. A wasps' nest on the roof, and a crack in the ceiling for them to drop into the room.

I'd previously got nothing against wasps. They didn't sting if you left them alone. A point to reflect upon, as I lay wide eyed through the long night, nauseous and feverish, pulse racing madly from all those stings. Trying to shove a piece of paper into the crack wasn't leaving them alone.

They weren't there by accident, of course. After so many years, when I'd lovingly filled it with books and paintings and the incense of wood smoke, I was selling the house. I had betrayed its trust, and it had summoned those wasps against me.

The rustling and nibbling said it all. We don't haunt places. They haunt us.

TIBBET'S RIDE

B UILT like a tank, in brown-belted raincoat, woollen stockings and brogues, head ramrod stiff and eyes unflinching, Frau Goering (as good a name as any) strode every day to and from the shops. An atom bomb up her arse wouldn't have made any difference.

Her other walk was up the Hill, where she always turned right at the Green Man, so allowing me, at a safe distance, to continue my stroll by the Heath as far as Tibbet's Corner.

Incidentally, Mr Tibbet, highwayman and footpad, was supposed to have been hanged on that spot. Fact is, Mr Tibbet never existed, but he should have done. There was his monument, frock coat, tricorne hat, flintlock in hand, amid the circling traffic. That's history for you.

Fact or fiction, he wouldn't know busy Tibbet's Ride today. But I knew that brown-belted raincoat and the plod of a fat Reichsmarshall coming up the side of the Heath.

Where was a gibbet when you wanted one?

CELTIC FRINGE

'SHAME about the parade.' The blurred city skyline was dotted with those old rooftop water tanks, or beehives collecting the grimy pollen off street and subway. Saint Patrick's Day in the rain.

'Ah!' Eamon our janitor lived on top of the block. 'But they're not what they were in my day!' He added a drop of the hard stuff to our coffee and lit a joint that filled the room with peat smoke.

'You'll know of the Hill of Tara,' he went on, 'sacred site of the ancient kings of Ireland, and of Brian Boru, greatest of them all. He, who played the famous Irish harp that you can see on every bottle of Guinness.'

Another drop of the hard stuff, and he started to sing, 'If You Ever Go Across the Sea to Ireland,' unless it was 'Danny Boy'.

Going back down the stairs was much more difficult than going up. So where was the bloody elevator? Where I'd left it, broken down again.

I knew there was something.

OPEN WIDE

IT sounded bad enough from the waiting room as the dentist dug out Lisa's deeply impacted molar, piece by tiny piece. It was her first day out in years.

I knew Lisa when she was a children's book illustrator and doing very well. That was before the agoraphobia kicked in and the work dried up. God knows what deeper psychosis had caused it. What must it be like to sit in that room, day in day out, year in year out, with your pills and your vodka, everything falling apart, dust and grime that made you cough and sneeze, and terrified to feel the fresh air and the sun upon your face. We literally had to drag her out to my car for that jolly trip to the dentist.

Back home, Lisa bawled through her butchered jaw, 'I want a drink!'

'You've had enough,' Tom bawled back from somewhere. He hadn't worked in years either.

They needed each other to yell at.

LITTLE OTTO

'*I do wish* you wouldn't call me that,' Elizabeth protested as we drove past fields of sugar cane, cows munching at their fringes with a bovine indifference to heat.

'Sorry darling,' Sylvia replied absently. I'd joined them for their holiday in the sun, a harmless male to help out.

Back on the beach, Elizabeth dug her sunshade into the sand while Sylvia and I stripped down for a swim. At the line of buoys she handed me the mask and snorkel and gave me a salty little kiss.

Through the mask, I spotted a baby octopus tuck himself into a crevice of rock till you wouldn't know he was there. What you could do without any bones!

Elizabeth's trouble was too many bones. She threw down her book. 'I saw the two of you snogging out there.'

'Lizzie darling, it was just a bit of fun.'

'Fun!' Elizabeth choked, trying to run up the beach in her flip-flops. 'And I *do wish* you wouldn't call me that.'

IN MEMORIAM

A sharp little nip on my big toe made me jump, and from under the bed sheet came the long bristling whiskers and little black shining eyes of a field mouse. He raised himself on my chest, chocolate brown fur on top, snow white underneath. He'd never seen a human before; I'd never been so close to a mouse. We regarded each other at leisure. Back on the floor, ambling not scampering, he went in search of other things to explore.

Like, my bag. Stiff, cold and weary after a long day's travel, I reached in it for my keys and touched something soft and limp.

Smothered by my pyjamas, little eyes now shut tight, tiny feet upturned in death, he'd said goodbye forever to the pine scented woods and rolling fields of sunflowers for the grey gritty corner of my street.

God rest his soul. And if he didn't have one, none of us did.

BLUE NOTE

'ALL right,' Henry said to Harriet's request. 'If you twist my arm.' I'd like to see her try. Henry was built like a heavyweight, though he didn't play Rachmaninov with the gloves on.

A useful guest at her dinner parties, he got up from the table and padded across to Harriet's waiting baby grand. Late Brahms this time, the notes falling like autumn raindrops as she served coffee and passed round the chocolate mints.

'Great stuff, Henry!' I applauded. 'Now how about some Blues!' We'd had great fun after one of his town hall recitals when I'd joined him at the keyboard to have a go at Cow Cow Boogie, till the caretaker chucked us out.

Henry's face lit up. It met Harriet's stony gaze. He'd better be going.

I drove him to the station. 'Any more recitals coming up?' Henry shook his head. His agent had dropped him. A scholarship and three years at the Royal College of Music were not enough.

Even for a chocolate mint.

JUMBO JET

'WAKE up, sleepy head!' Sarah was banging on my door. She didn't believe in jet lag.

'Come on, slow coach!' she beckoned from the serene and golden head of the reclining Buddha in the temple of Wat Po while I blinked at the inscrutable words of wisdom on his two big flat feet.

After lunch I hit the sack till the brazen hoot of a trumpet woke me again. Down in the heat-exhausted street a little bow-legged man in dhoti and turban walked ahead of a lumbering elephant, a box half filled with junk across his neck. Another hoot and they were gone.

'Hey, you'll never guess what I saw!' I greeted Sarah when they all got back from the Floating Market. She smiled, and sat down to supper with this other guy.

Still with him on the flight home and waiting in the cheerless baggage hall. Two items came round on the carousel, his and hers.

She turned and waved. 'Have fun.'

BON APPETIT

IN the Middle Ages, I said, they'd have burnt Gustave at the stake for witchcraft. With a gargoyle for a face, he lived in a filthy hovel down the hill from the village with a family of poor mangy cats, his gruesome familiars.

Actually, it was whispered that Gustave sometimes had one of them for supper. He spoke in squeaks and grunts, as though he had a piece of claw lodged in his throat. Not that he ever had much to say, working all alone down at the sludge tank till the day he died.

'Listen,' somebody said. 'It's stopped.' Me, or the storm that had rumbled away over the hills? Whichever it was, it was time for my friends to depart.

After they'd gone, one last ember still glowed among the ashes of the fire, the heart going out of the old house again, soon to be shuttered and bolted through another long winter.

Places can get just as lonely as people, who could skin a cat for the pot.

END GAME

YAPPY Popeyes was a large bug-eyed, bandy-legged beetle, unless he was a Chihuahua, a breed of so-called dog from Mexico. One of those famous hats would have snuffed him out. You could hold him in both hands, though I wouldn't have advised it. He crapped and snapped at the same time. He'd just thrown up.

'Poor darling.' Pat clutched him to her bosom. 'It's the heat.'

It wasn't the only thing. Corinne's old cat ambled down the garden path looking for a spot of shade. Yappy Popeyes now began to tremble and to emit a half strangled wail. Pat clutched him even closer to her bosom. 'Can you get rid of that cat!'

Never mind the cat. There was a crash from inside the house. Caliban had broken loose again. God knows what sort of a dog he was, but he thundered through Corinne's garden door, all shaggy hair and dribble, heading straight for Pat.

Well, not actually for her.

DINNER DATE

EMBRACEABLE You by George Gershwin. One of my favourites, seated at the baby grand in a corner of the big colonial dining room, doors and windows open to the boom of surf at midday, to the blood-red sun spilling into the sea come dinnertime, and me watching her watching me across the floor.

I'd seen her down by the pool, on her own and reading a book, no spring chicken but with a body that still had something to give. Now, one of a jolly dinner party, hair streaked with just a few strands of grey and brushed back over her ears, and in a silvery dress that sparkled as she moved, she laughed and chatted on cue, while watching me watching her across the floor.

Embraceable You. With a scraping of chairs they all got up to go, still laughing and chatting, and with one last glance over her shoulder for the two of us to remember.

JOLLY ROGER

BANG. Roger's cracker contained a skull and cross-bones paper hat and a joke. Why don't owls make love in the rain? Because it's too wet to woo.

Wendy had invited me to the office Christmas party, but get me out of there. And never mind the rain. I strode along to the Emperor Concerto. Now I remembered. Musical nicknames. A nice little item for the next edition of *In Classical Mood*. 'Emperor' Concerto, 'Raindrop' Prelude, 'Moonlight' Sonata. In the old days, a few words with Roger and I'd have the copy on his desk before you could say Dmitri Shostakovich.

That was before Wendy. She'd arrived as his temp. His personal assistant now, and you needed a bloody passport to see him.

At Hammersmith Broadway, a taxi pulled up at the lights with a splash. Was that her inside, next to a skull and crossbones paper hat, somewhat askew?

The lights turned green. 'Where to now, guv?'

Wapping. Execution Dock.

BON VOYAGE

SID and Edna stepped off the train, looking like they'd landed on Mars. 'Bit different from Lewisham,' I said cheerily, as I drove them from the station.

Their daughter had booked them into my room upstairs, a present for mum and dad on their silver wedding. The South of France, though not the Côte d'Azur.

And not a whisper out of them till next morning. 'The noise of them bloody frogs.' Edna's voice. 'Kept me awake all night. And bitten all over.' Sid said something. Edna again. 'Go on, finish the bottle, why don't you?' Sid said something else.

Real-life violence isn't the choreographed stuff you see on screen, it's clumsy and helpless, just the sound of it, and the silence afterwards is even worse.

They wouldn't let me drive them back to the station, so I left them at the bus stop, in what little shade there was, a black eye, a plaster, and the big brown suitcase between them.

BUNNY CLUB

I'D only seen them for a moment, but as soon as she got on the train at Earl's Court, I recalled those two buck teeth, resting on her lower lip to give her an expression of, how to put it, glum content.

All of twenty years ago, the dating agency had put us in touch, and we agreed to meet at Holborn station. She'd be wearing a lucky rabbit's foot in the lapel of her coat.

Up the escalator and there she was, with her lucky rabbit's foot and those two buck teeth. Why waste each other's time. Straight back down the other escalator and back into the next train, the peristaltic wobble of pipes and wires along the tunnel wall keeping one big lump of shit on the move.

Suzie Rose. How long, I wonder, did she wait for me on that shameful day.

She got off the train again at Green Park without a hint of recognition. Of course not, you bastard.

For a second time, forgive me Suzie if you can.

LAUGHING SAL

THROUGH the salt-caked windows in the basement of Cliff House, Diana stared out at the stretch of wet promenade to the hump of Seal Rock. She turned back to the dusty clutter of pinball tables and miniature cranes dangling over heaps of tarnished trinkets and charms. The graveyard of a penny arcade.

Not quite dead. I dropped a dime into a small organ or calliope. A wheezy pair of bellows fed pipes that suddenly blared out The Stars and Stripes Forever, as you'd never heard it before nor ever wanted to again.

Laughing Sal was still alive as well. A limbless torso in blue and white polka dot smock and a wicked shiny face beneath a ginger wig. For another dime she began to shake and shudder and to laugh and scream inside her glass case. You could be drowning out there, reaching for the slippery sides of Seal Rock, while Sal went on laughing and screaming fit to bust.

'Some bloody holiday,' Diana bawled even louder.

LAST RITES

IT wasn't our funeral, but somehow we'd got stuck in the middle of a convoy of big black limousines and shunted back to what must have been the home of the deceased.

From our little car we watched them pass through the gates and disappear inside. 'Come on,' I said to Jill, 'I reckon they owe us one, and with that crowd they'll never notice us.'

Cognac, Armagnac, it hit the spot. 'They should do a Michelin Guide to some of the cemeteries they have over here,' I said. 'Crosses for interest, skulls for atmosphere.'

Tables were laden with food and wine. 'The funeral baked meats did coldly furnish forth the marriage table.' I smacked my lips. 'Hamlet .'

'Alas, poor Yorick.' Jill waved her glass. 'Like one of your skulls.'

I handed her a plate and fork. 'Better eat something.'

'A Funeral baked bean?' She collapsed with laughter and slid to the floor with a bowl of mayonnaise.

'I think I'm going to be sick,' she said next.

HAPPY DAYS

'WHAT a game, eh!' He joined me on the seat, a white carnation in his buttonhole and clutching a bottle of bubbly. 'Like some?'

'Not your wedding, is it?' I asked, as they gathered noisily and happily outside the big gothic house in the park popular for such receptions.

'Not this time,' he chuckled. 'You been married?'

I wiped the neck of the bottle. 'Divorced.' You can sometimes speak more easily with strangers than with friends. 'It's love affairs that kill you,' I began.

'Terry!' A no-nonsense young lady with floral hat and black shiny handbag stood a little way down the path. 'What you doin' here?' She beckoned impatiently. 'Come on, it's goin' to pour in a minute.'

The sky had turned the colour of a deep and wounding bruise, and with it came that rare and passing fragrance as the first swollen raindrops soaked into warm dry ground.

Terry clambered to his feet, crushed out his cigarette.

'What a game, eh!'

BABY FACE

'CAN you take Baby for a walk?' Beth pleaded as she mopped up in the car. She was into pet therapy, but five minutes with Baby and you'd be ready to jump off the Brooklyn Bridge.

Still, up here where the birdies sang in the trees things might be a bit less frenetic. So up verdant Chestnut Street, round the corner, and wow! A large gothic residence with more than a touch of Psycho about it stared back through empty windows from behind dark trees.

Stand very still and listen for the ghostly chime of the clock at the foot of the stairs, the creak of a floorboard up in the attic where the rocking horse tipped gently to and fro at the touch of an unseen hand.

Someone else had gone very quiet, crouched by the side of the road. Baby looked hopefully up at me, a super-annuated, incontinent, off-white poodle in need of a bit of love.

'Come on, for God's sake.' I tugged at his lead before anybody else saw what we'd just done.

NORTHERN LINE

ONE quick glance was enough to tell us that we ticked every box, looks, demeanour, personality, sensuality, ten out of ten. The yin and the yang of two people trapped in the sanitised white light of the tube train and in such a state of shocked recognition that we dared not look again, nor hardly move, nor breathe.

Warren Street, Goodge Street. Supposing one of us got up to go? Tottenham Court Road, Leicester Square. How long could this go on, this bubble of enchantment while the rest of the world came and went all around us?

Waterloo, the bubble burst and we both jumped up like a pair of marionettes. She stood waiting by the doors, her back half turned to me, and if I'd reached out and touched her we'd have blown every fuse from High Barnet to Morden.

Down onto the platform, up the steps, along the winding corridor, onto the escalator.

The milling crowd at the top.

BLACK COFFEE

EDITH said she could tell everything about a person by their handwriting. Look at mine. Those big pendulous loops told her I had a wild imagination. They were something she'd like to discuss at this international symposium on handwriting and would I go as her guest.

You couldn't make it up, I thought, gazing through the window of Tonopah Joe's Truck Stop, where we took a break on the long drive back to the airport. Cinder-grey hills ringed the horizon, dust devils spun in the air, and a heap of rocks, smoothed and polished by sand and wind, now roasted under the noonday sun like giant coffee beans.

And what of Tonopah Joe, a dwarf in baseball cap, orange sweatshirt, tartan shorts and sneakers, or a Nibelung of the Wild West who crept out at night to chip away at those fabulous beans.

Edith took a sip of the hot black brew in her cup. 'Good coffee,' she said.

'The best,' I agreed.

CREEPY CRAWLIES

'DON'T the females eat their mates?' asked a young man with acne and a squint.

'Sometimes, Derek.' Kate's hands were full with Judy from Trinidad, a large lady with eight legs dangling like hairy fingers. Open Day at the Insect House, though as Kate reminded us, spiders are arachnids not insects.

So what of this arachnophobia, this primal horror lodged so deep in our collective unconscious? Hard to say, with the tiny money spider and her promise of good luck. Easier to understand with the kind we sometimes find in the bath or kitchen sink. Bloated grey bellies suspended between eight long segmented legs and a manic turn of speed, when not spinning cocoons in dark corners, waiting motionless, eyes unblinking, for the moment to pounce and bite and paralyse and gorge.

Kate placed Judy back in her glass case, her tropic enclave, where Derek could take a closer look. With his squint how many legs could he count on her? Sixteen?

Try him with a millipede.

HEAVENS ABOVE

UNDER the anodyne white light of the chapel, electronic organ music oozed from somewhere and mum's coffin moved slowly towards the curtains at the back. She believed that when she died she'd go straight to heaven and into the arms of Jesus. The vicar had just said so too.

So what about the Bible and the Creed? They spoke of a Judgement Day when Christ would return in glory to call us back from the grave and admit us to heaven or cast us into hell. And where would that leave my mum's small heap of ashes? Once you started, the doubts, the questions, just kept on coming.

Afterwards, I thanked the vicar and shook his hand. What did he really think and believe? He'd been doing it for so long maybe he didn't care any more. Let him get home to his tea.

And let my mum rest in the arms of Jesus. Or whatever.

DELHI BELLY

'MONSOON?' Geraldine scoffed. 'Rubbish!' Okay, but with the sound of that rain I could hardly think to play Scrabble. 'Otiose?' she snapped. 'That's not a word!'

She'd invited me on one of her trips buying gems and jewellery for her boutique. We'd stay with Florrie and have such fun.

'What about a drink?' The chink of ice in Geraldine's glass was half the fun. Fine, those ice cubes from the kitchen freezer should keep her happy. Scotch on the rocks for one.

'Poor lassie,' Florrie said in the morning as we watched the ambulance depart. 'I'm sure it's nothing I gave you.' Florrie lit another cigarette from the stub of the old, the last gasp of the Raj, and clapped her hands at a fat old crow perched on the window sill. They helped to keep down the cockroaches. This one dipped a wing as it took off, a bellyful of cockroach.

The aircraft dipped a wing over the fuzz of lights below. 'Drink, sir?'

'A whisky and soda perhaps.'

'Ice?'

'No, thanks.'

YULE TIDE

IN the fading light of day, seagulls flapped and squabbled and churned up the water in a large rock pool. They didn't know how lucky they were.

Back in the darkened car park, fairy lights from a dozen windows winked and blinked at us with a clockwork apathy.

'Think of them in there,' I said to Jennie. 'Half past three in the afternoon, hot, bloated, fartless, the Queen on the telly, a row in the kitchen.' I turned the key in the ignition. 'I know, I've been through a few of 'em.'

Not any more. A bracing walk by the sea and back to smoked salmon, lightly steamed potatoes and asparagus, lemon sorbet, and a nicely chilled bottle of bubbly.

'Hungry?' I asked, as we breezed along, just before the engine coughed, spluttered and died. I wrenched on the hand brake as the first gust of wind and rain came out of black night.

Jennie pointed to the fuel gauge. Empty. 'When,' she asked, 'shall I open the champers?'

HALF CUT

'CAN you take over for a minute?' he begged. At the corner of the alley, in grubby vest and shorts, Julian was down on his hands and knees, gripping a pair of scissors.

He rented a studio in his friend Yvonne's house. She'd gone away for the weekend, leaving him with instructions to feed her prize Burmese cat Mistinguett. The latter was on heat, and when she started her infernal caterwauling, Julian threw her out. Come Monday morning, he was crawling round the village trying to lure her back home, making the sound that Yvonne made with her scissors as she cut up little slices of fish for Mistinguett.

Right now you'd never guess that Julian's paintings sold for mega bucks in Paris, London and New York. If I found Mistinguett perhaps he'd give me one. And perhaps he wouldn't, by lunchtime back at the Bar du Chateau and on his fifth pastis.

I turned the corner. 'All right,' he bawled, 'go fuck yourself!'

Snip snip.

OLD PAL

HE made me think of the ancient Egyptian god Anubis with his long pointed snout and pointed ears. But Miriam named him Pal on account of the tins of dog food she bought him together with a bowl. He'd come sniffing around on our first day at the beach and he'd filled out nicely in the last few days. And while Debbie and I frolicked in the sea, Miriam sat on the beach in her spot of shade, plump legs stuck out, red where the sun had briefly touched them, with Pal by her side.

Night came quickly in those latitudes. Across the Bay, the darkening outline of Basse Terre ended with the blip of one small island, and back on the beach Pal was settling down next to his bowl. He'd be waiting in the morning.

'Hurry up!' Debbie called to her sister. 'We've still got all the packing to do.' We were off again first thing tomorrow.

I pressed Miriam's hand and whispered, 'He'll be alright.'

EN VACANCES

SWIFTS and swallows crowned brightest day with little shrieks of joy as we drove through Pont Saint Esprit, Bridge of the Holy Spirit. Dora clapped her hands. 'What a lovely name, dear!' Reg swiped at a fly.

Auntie Dora and Uncle Reg, who used to send me socks for Christmas. I hardly remembered them but they'd remembered me, or Dora had. Now on a coach tour and with a few hours to spare they'd dug me out. I'd better take them somewhere.

'Take your cap off, dear!' In the gloom of the chapel, painted columns rose to a vaulted ceiling of midnight blue patterned with stars, and candles flickered before the statue of the Virgin.

'It's all so lovely.' Dora reached for my hand and whispered, 'Thank you for taking us out like this. Reg doesn't say much, but I know he's loving it too.'

Back in the car, cap back on and nose starting to peel, Reg swiped at a fly.

TIME CHECK

WE sat for a moment, still trying to get our heads around it.

All of fifty years since we'd parted. Either of us could have been anywhere. Yet there we were, in the same compartment of the same tube train on the same day of the year. Millions to one against, must be.

'Did you know it was me?' she asked, as we toyed with the coffee that neither of us wanted.

'Yes.' Grey-haired and wrinkled now, but the same girl forever and a day.

'How are you anyway?'

'Fine, thanks.'

'You're looking well.'

'And you.'

We looked out the cafe window, anywhere but at each other. The chasm of time was too great to span.

'Still working hard?'

'On and off.' I glanced at my watch.

'You're in a hurry.'

'A bit.'

'Me too.'

Another silence, as heavy as uranium, then with a scrape of chairs we both got up.

'I'll pay.'

'No, let me.'

COMMAND PERFORMANCE

IT was quite a shock to see Bob's face staring back at me from a page of the newspaper. For years, he'd been squatting outside the bank, strategically placed for a handout, and when I dropped a few coins in his cap he always had a cheerful word for me, while Sam nuzzled his cold wet nose into my hand.

So what had Bob done to attract this sudden fame? He'd been convicted of begging while living off benefits in a smart council house.

Okay, he'd sucked me in, but it was a good performance, out there with Sam under a dirty old blanket, come rain come shine, half starved, chewing on a bun, with the dregs of cold tea in a plastic cup, before going home to champagne and caviar, or something of the sort.

And something in between, I'd say, where he'd gone to stay for a while as a guest of Her Majesty.

Though Sam hadn't been invited.

WATER SPORTS

MILLICENT screamed. She'd disturbed a tarantula spider under a piece of wood, not some tropical monster but the real thing, native to the Midi, though still of a healthy size.

Always something up with Millicent. She wanted to work up a tan, so here we were, among the dry stone terraces, the parched rows of lavender and withered vines, the dead and dying almond trees, cracked and twisted under the weight of heat, the abandoned farmhouses, when the land got too hard to work.

But wait. Close by one of them, a pair of wooden shutters set into the hillside opened upon a large cistern of crystal clear water. I could have jumped straight in. Just don't let those shutters close on you again. Nothing to cling onto in there, no one to hear you, no one to know, up there in the lonely sun-baked hills.

Her face now a lobster red, Millicent kicked at the empty water bottle.

I beckoned. 'Come over here and take a dip.'

RED ALERT

HERPES Zoster isn't the name of some ancient fire god, it's shingles, though the pain is like being burnt alive.

'Oh! You poor boy!' Rosalind said. 'You should be home in bed.' I know, but she wasn't there to tuck me in, which is why I brought my next lot of copy to their offices, just to see her.

Not for long. The red light by her phone flashed angrily. Rosalind grabbed pen and paper and rushed into Toby's office. He'd bawled and bullied his way to the top of the magazine business and couldn't stop now. That wasn't all.

The shame and the humiliation, her weekly date with Toby, the hotel dinner and after, then to shout at her like that, for everyone to hear.

Back at her desk, Rosalind made a big thing of blowing her nose and tried a brave little smile. 'We're a fine pair, aren't we?'

Yes, and why couldn't we have had a go? At least I'd still be there when she woke up.

TRAVELLING LIGHT

HE lurched down the aisle of the compartment, unwashed, unshaven, clutching a black plastic bin bag and gripping under one sweaty armpit a small dog with a piece of string tied round its neck in place of a lead.

We cringed as he passed by, and heaved a sigh of relief when he found a seat, shoved the dog between his feet and began to rummage around in the bag, creating plenty of space for himself

The train meantime had gathered speed, leaning into the track as it followed the broad silvery curve of the river and flooding the compartment with light. Gone was the watercolour world of meadow, wood and stream. The sun now ruled from a cloudless sky over vineyard and orchard, pine and cypress and dusty olive grove.

Closer to hand, eyes closed to the sway and rhythm of the train, one small dog was cradled in his master's arms.

The world on a string.

FRENCH KISS

'THE girl in the boulangerie is quite nice,' Gordon muttered.

I'm surprised he'd noticed. He was out of his house, round the shops and back again before you could say, 'Bonjour'. What had induced him, a solitary bachelor, to move abroad and to our village in the first place? He couldn't speak a word of the language, and those stacks of coins by his window weren't the hoard of a miserly Scotsman. They were the change from his shopping he didn't know what to do with.

'Funny you should say that,' I replied. 'She was asking about you.'

Gordon turned an incandescent red beneath his Caledonian whiskers. He swilled the wine round his glass. He put it to his nose. 'I fear,' he stuttered in his confusion, 'it is still a little t-too young.'

Speaking of age, girl was pushing it. She'd been around, and handling those baguettes, still warm from the oven, probably turned her on.

'Shall I give her your love?' I asked. 'And kisses?'

LOST LADY

'EXCUSE me.' She sat on a low garden wall with her shopping bag. The voice was as fragile as the rest of her. 'Do you know where we are? I've forgotten.'

I waved a hand. 'Do you recognise any of this?'

She shook her head, then raised her own thin, blue-veined hand against the sun. 'I say, isn't that a beautiful rose!'

The creamy white bloom was tinged with crimson, a floral menstruation. 'Yes, and just down the road there's a bush of lavender. I love watching the bees, especially the bumble bees, buzzing and bobbing from flower to flower.'

'I can see,' she said, 'you haven't lost your sense of wonder. You must be a happy man.'

I shook my head too. 'The more you think and see and feel, the more you can get hurt.'

'All the same, talking to you has made me feel so much better!'

I smiled. 'Me too.'

The trouble with conversations is that you easily forget what started them.

SMOKE SIGNALS

THAT boulder must be a meteorite, black and shiny and of an unimaginable weight. God knows how it got to stand at the corner of the Rue de l'Horloge, where my neighbour, face of a wrinkled walnut, woolly stockings and clogs, sat on fine summer days and watched the world go by.

I awoke each morning to the squeak and groan as she opened her shutters, and settled down each evening to the squeak and groan as she closed them again. The smoke from her chimney was a different matter, a yellowish cloud with a whiff of "ordures". I might have complained to the Mairie, but returning one springtime I didn't need to. As impossible as it seemed, the shutters squeaked and groaned, the chimney smoked no more, and the meteorite was an empty throne.

I looked in vain in the cemetery for her grave. But seen from my terrace, as swifts and swallows wheeled and screamed in the radiant evening light, how black that chimney appeared.

Spontaneous combustion. What else.

BEAR FACTS

'OKAY!' Madame Butterfly, as I called her, tapped on my bedroom door, saw me in my pyjamas and fled.

Still in them, I was out of the hotel and across the street, where that old black man was slumped on the sidewalk with his bits and pieces, including a teddy bear, one ear half off and big button eyes, wide with appeal. 'What,' they asked, 'what is to become of me?'

Two bucks and he was mine. Behind us, as the song said, little cable cars climbed half way to the stars, to the top of Russian Hill and a view over the Bay to Alcatraz Island. And with a small strip of cloth above each eye, unusual for a bear, I'd just met Eyebrows Alcatraz, the bear who got away.

Next thing, the hotel elevator took us down instead of up, where Madame Butterfly waited with more fresh linen.

She'd seen the pyjamas, so it must be the bear. 'Okay!' she gasped, leaving me and Eyebrows to climb half way to the stars, as far as the second floor.

NEEDLE WORK

TO get round it I must step off the pavement onto the road and walk past a line of parked cars. Why the hell should I have to?

Prince Albert, I believe, introduced the Christmas tree to England. Today huge plantations of young fir trees were destined to be uprooted and cut off by those roots, trussed up for the shops and, like this poor victim now in front of me, placed in the corner of some hot and stuffy room, bedecked with fairy lights and trinkets. And when the fun and games were over, chucked into the street for someone else to dispose of, or not.

With my shoe, I began to shove its desiccated corpse into the curb between two of those parked cars, leaving behind a heap of brown needles, like a pool of blood.

A faint residual scent of resin, of pine woods in dappled sunlight, hung in the damp, chill winter air. Even in death it tried to please.

LATIN LESSON

THE sun hit us like a fist as we stepped out of the church. The massive hump of the Dent de Rez, highest point of the region, loomed over us and over the stony landscape with its scattered and abandoned almond trees, cracked and twisted in attitudes of death. The word crucified came to mind.

'By the way,' I said to Priscilla, 'the letters INRI over that big Crucifix in the church stand for the Latin words *Iesus Nazarenus Rex Iudaeorum,* Jesus of Nazareth King of the Jews. There was no letter J in the Latin alphabet.'

'Like another one?' I didn't give her time to say no. 'SPQR, proud legend of the Roman legions, *Senatus Populusque Romanus,* the Senate and People of Rome.' The *que,* I explained, was the Latin for "and".

Through her sunglasses, Priscilla was watching a buzzard high in the deep blue dome of sky, wings outstretched and circling lazily on a thermal of air. 'Thank you, Mr Clever Clogs.'

'Anytime.'

COPY CAT

'THAT'S new,' I said. Van Gogh's Sunflowers was propped against the television in front of The Hay Wain and The Fighting Temeraire. In retirement Oliver made copies of famous paintings. At the door to his flat you had to squeeze past a framed Mona Lisa, and in the bathroom you took a piss with The Laughing Cavalier.

'Yes,' he replied. 'All that impasto.' Oliver wiggled his thumb about, as though applying paints to the canvas. 'The Fauves owed a hell of a lot to Van Gogh. Matisse, Vlaminck, Braque. That crowd.'

'The wild beasts.' Pam edged her way into the room balancing three plates of sausage and mash. 'That's what *fauves* means in French, dickhead.'

Not how I'd describe Picasso, a black tom of stupendous girth. I fed him a piece of sausage and watched him expand some more. 'So, what's next?' I asked. 'Guernica?'

'Christ!' Oliver spluttered through a mouthful of mashed potato. 'Have you seen the size of it!'

I winked at Picasso. He blinked at me.

DOG DAYS

THEY call it "la canicule" or "little dog", a heat wave that comes with the appearance in the night sky of Cirius or the Dog Star.

In other words, the dog days, when canines just lie around and pant and scratch their fleas.

Except for the pampered Pekinese at the restaurant, who whimpered and yapped the whole time. Nor was it the heat but another dog, about ten sizes larger, with a coat like a Persian rug, flopped out beneath another table.

It was going to take a lot to shift him, but the whimpering and yapping did it in the end. He yanked himself to his feet, toppling over the table and sending a cascade of plates, glasses and cutlery crashing to the patio floor. It nearly ended in a fight, and not between the dogs.

So much for a romantic evening under the stars. Perhaps that very bright one over to the west was Cirius. Closer to hand, the hot dry hills withdrew into the night.

TUNNEL VISION

WHOOPS! The train gave a lurch and she fell back into her seat, holding onto a carton of coffee, a packet of biscuits and a bag of crisps, chubby face, chubby all over.

'You should have seen the queue,' she said to her friend, struggling with the packet of biscuits. 'You'd think they didn't want us to eat them!' The packet broke open scattering biscuits everywhere. She gathered them up and stuffed one into her mouth.

'What time do we get in, anyway?' she asked, poking crumbs into the side of it. She fiddled with her wrist-watch. 'Do we put it backwards or forwards? I always forget.'

She crunched on a crisp. 'So what do you fancy tonight? Indian or Chinese?' She giggled. 'Remember that vindaloo? Talk about the trots!'

The train slowed for a moment, with a fleeting glimpse of Calais town hall, before it entered the tunnel.

She caught her reflection in the lighted window, face suddenly slack and vacant, the crisps all gone.

DARK DAYS

'TAKE a look in the room at the back,' Bunty said. She'd bought the old house in the alley called the Grande Rue that had been empty longer than anyone in the village could remember.

'Got to go back to Blighty for a couple of weeks.' She handed me what looked like the keys to the Bastille.

Generations of woodworm had broken their teeth on the door to that room, and when I'd shoved it open a few inches I'd have been a fool to strike a match. The air was something else. Festoons of cobweb hung across one small window, rotten floorboards threatened to drop me into an oubliette. And in the dim half light, what the hell was that, propped up at the back of the blackened fireplace.

'Marble plaque?' A retired headmistress, Bunty was used to asking questions. 'What's it doing there?'

'Don't ask me, but I'd take a closer look at that fire-place, just in case.'

Tiny beads of sweat ringed the fur on Bunty's upper lip. A warm day for tweeds. 'In case of what?'

BOTTOMS UP

A hint of creme de menthe, I thought, savouring Jim's latest concoction. 'Cocktails began with Prohibition, didn't they?'

They went back further than that, Jim said. The first so-called cocktail, a bit like a mint julep, was probably invented in Kentucky in 1806. And some people say, the name might have been inspired by an Aztec Princess Xochitl and her elixir of love.

Aztec princess! Elixir of love! I grabbed Jim's phone. 'Hallo, Fiona?' My editor, sharp and neurotic and looking like the figure in that painting, The Scream.

'Good news, Fiona, Jim's fixed my computer so I'm back on track with my text. And get this, he also makes cocktails and he's writing a book about them. Interested? You know, Manhattan, Bloody Mary, Brass Monkey, Zombie, Screwdriver, Rusty Nail, Hanky Panky, Between the Sheets, Strip and Go Naked, Harvey Wallbanger. What? Wall, Fiona, as in bricks. Banger, as in sausage.'

The stupid bitch hung up. I pointed to Jim's silver shaker. 'Any more of that stuff?'

POST SCRIPT

IF you're in a hole, stop digging. Like all the best advice it's very hard to take on board. Compulsively, I went on adding a word here, deleting one there, getting nowhere fast.

Through my window, the still tender and unsullied leaves on the trees shivered in the chill unseasonal wind. And down the road was that abandoned car with a wad of soggy parking tickets stuck under the windscreen wiper and the little striped tiger left on top of the dashboard, button eyes raised hopelessly to the world. I had to go the long way round to the shops to avoid them.

Why did I feel such pity for inanimate objects? Maybe that's what I should try to write about next time and dig myself another hole.

With a superhuman effort, I finally stopped and stood up, cold and stiff. Time in any case to get down to the shops, the long way round.

Bread, soup, fish fingers.